MOO-
I LOVE

Abrams Books
for Young Readers
NEW YORK

MOO, YOU!

TOM LICHTENHELD

AMY KROUSE ROSENTHAL

Moo-moo, I love you.

I love you no matter

Good m●●-d . . .

your m●●-d.

Bad m●●-d...

Sad m●●-d . . .   Silly m●●-d.

I love when we share our favorite things . . .

pizza with
extra moo-zzarella,

and groovin' to m●●-sic.

I love it when you turn our house into a m●●-seum.

I love to see you sch-m●●-zing with your friends...

you're obviously a good

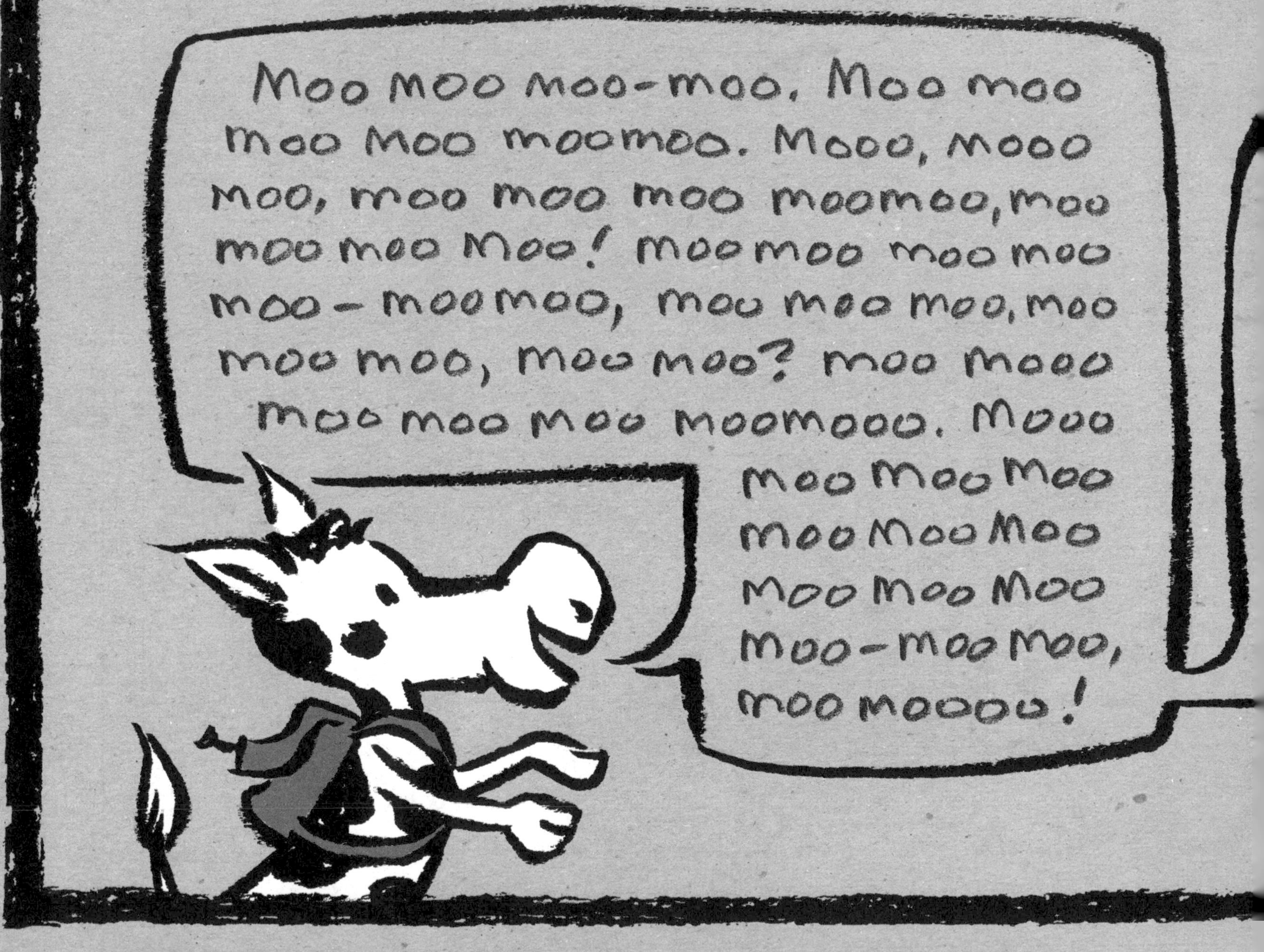

com-m●●-nicator!

My love for you is as big as a ...

moo-se!

I'd walk a thousand
miles for you . . .

At the end of the day,
I love giving you a big

S·MOO

I'd jump over
the m●●-n for you!

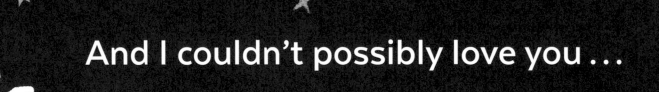

And I couldn't possibly love you . . .

...moo-er.

FOR AMY

IN LOVING MEMORY OF AMY KROUSE ROSENTHAL
—T.L.

The illustrations for this book were made with Pentel brush pen on
watercolor paper, with Photoshop color. Digital tweakage by Kristen Cella.

Library of Congress Control Number 2019957664

ISBN 978-1-4197-4706-9

Printed and bound in U.S.A.
10 9 8 7 6 5 4 3 2 1

Abrams Books for Young Readers are available at special discounts when purchased in quantity for
premiums and promotions as well as fundraising or educational use. Special editions can also be created to specification.
For details, contact specialsales@abramsbooks.com or the address below.

Abrams® is a registered trademark of Harry N. Abrams, Inc.

ABRAMS The Art of Books
195 Broadway, New York, NY 10007
abramsbooks.com

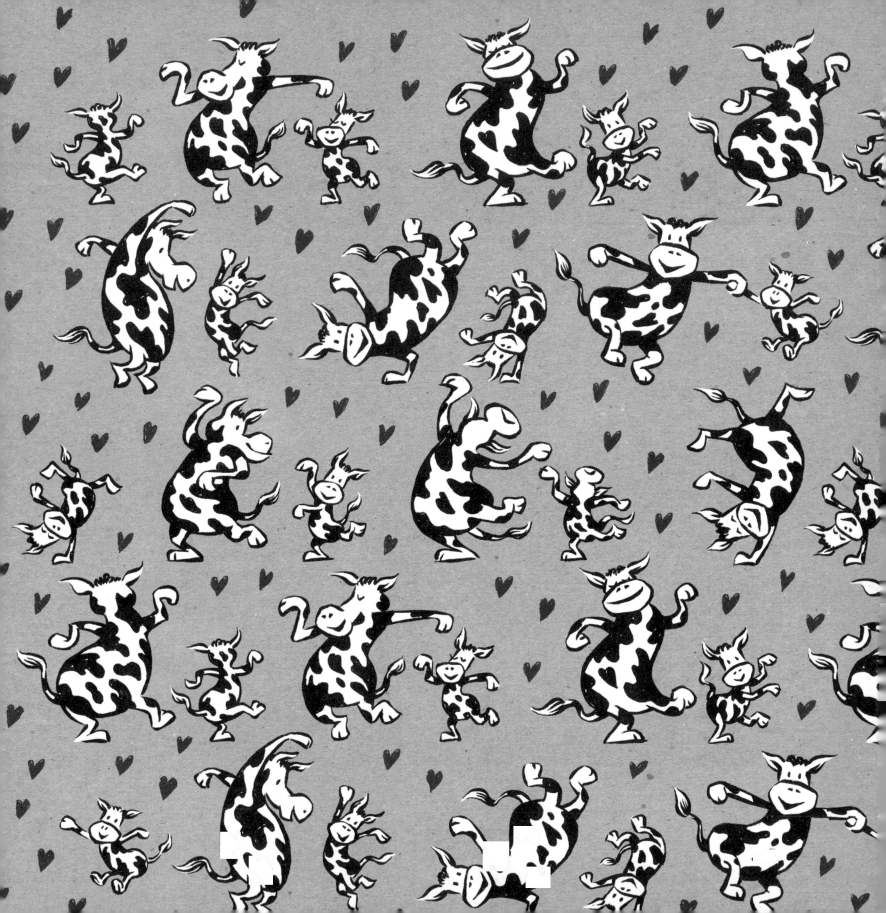